HECATE AND
HER DOGS

PAUL MORAND

HECATE AND HER DOGS

Translated from the French by
David Coward

PUSHKIN PRESS
LONDON

With thanks to Caroline de Moubray

Hecate and Her Dogs
First published in French as *Hécate et ses chiens* in 1954
© Flammarion 1954

English translation © David Coward 2009

Afterword © Umberto Pasti 2009
Afterword translation © Shaun Whiteside 2009

This edition first published in 2009 by

Pushkin Press
12 Chester Terrace
London NW1 4ND

ISBN 978 1 901285 80 2

All rights reserved. No part of this publication may be
reproduced, stored in a retrieval system or transmitted in
any form or by any means, electronic, mechanical,
photocopying, recording or otherwise,
without prior permission in writing from
Pushkin Press

Cover: *Hecate* 1795 William Blake
Tate Britain © Bridgeman Art Library

p 146 Hélène Soutzo Paul Nadar
© Ministère de la Culture
Médiathèque du Patrimoine Dist. RMN Paul Nadar

Frontispiece: Paul Morand 1935
© Rex Features Roger-Viollet

Set in 10½ on 13 Baskerville
and printed in Great Britain by TJ International Ltd
Padstow Cornwall

HECATE AND
HER DOGS

*Single, I caused chaos around me;
double, oh how much more so.*
    Helen, in *Faust Part II*, Goethe

ONCE I SHOOK the dust of the place from my boots swearing never to return. But now after all I shall be setting foot there again, though it was not of my choosing. A forced stopover means waiting for a connecting flight which will whisk me off tomorrow to a third continent. A continent a day—these days we wear seven-league boots.

We fly so fast I don't get much of a look at the first skyscrapers, we're over them, then we've overflown them, bowled along by the fury of the wind which adds its power to our four engines.

My eyes run on faster than my thoughts. Two hours ago I was in Paris and now here I am in Africa—in just the time it took to have lunch and read my paper. The ocean is spread out beneath my feet, over violet rocks lying on beds of waxy sand. The wind does not just pummel the waves, it shreds them; having no clouds on which to vent its spleen, angered by the mocking blue void, the rainless hurricane beats down mercilessly on spume and foam, and feathers the water; it rages against the plane which lowers its wing-flaps for the descent.

The airport is new to me. These asphalt roads weren't there thirty years ago. The town has grown up and grown bigger; I hardly recognise the place. It looks surprisingly young, the way we say old people do. It stacks its houses in storeys on the beach and its duros on its foreign-exchange counters. With my sixty-year-old eyes, I stare out at this corner of the world where I left my youth and spent the worst years of my life.

I

IT WAS THIRTY YEARS AGO and I had just arrived, after leaving my job with the Audit Office. I pounced on the country with missionary zeal, impatient to be getting on with the job, to put to good use the bitter lessons that a very old foreign money market was beginning to teach the finances of Europe, which had been dilapidated by the War. The currency of my own victorious country was in poor shape; the franc, suddenly weakened by the defection of its stable-mate, the pound sterling, would have to hold its own against a peseta which had made the most of the opportunities offered by neutrality to steal a march on both.

I was the representative of a bank whose status was almost as official as that of the State Bank. Paris left me on a loose rein, my callow illusions held out the promise of a significant financial role—starting as a novice I would quickly become a master of the craft; I would no longer just attend to my duties, I should do my Duty.

I would contribute to re-establishing a political and moral order which I intended to be wholly French.

I'd come to the wrong place. Accustomed to regular office hours, I could make nothing of a system of working which seemed to ape the Stock Exchange's saw-toothed graphs. Democratic changes were just beginning to take the downward turn which has yet to bottom out. The pace of business fell into step—no golden mean here; either a frenzy of activity on the exchanges, phones glued to ears, or the immobility of those standing guard over treasure in the form of assets frozen by fear and funds which were available but leery and unresponsive to any investment opportunity. Between these two extremes, quiet periods of unlimited leisure lasting perhaps for months during which my branch was little more than a letter box. Then all of a sudden, the millions are unleashed, a fever of speculation, panic flight from inflation, wrangles between giant players, tidal waves on a world scale which would keep me on my toes for a few days. Then it would all settle down again. At such times you couldn't have imagined anything more provincial than my little counting house clinging to a shore peopled by a throng of ghosts. The semi-colonial life led by the Europeans, their indolence, the fiction of their involvement in activities which earned them a crust, it all seemed a lie lived against a backdrop of sky-blue, the ephemeral decor of those who are just passing through.

I was surrounded by Consulate bickering and the squabbling of the bridge-players, my door was darkened by tottery retired gents, furtive drifters, or, murkier still, international conscientious objectors, political refugees, the accumulated flotsam thrown up by the late war, all waiting to be granted a nationality or, failing that, a passport. All of this created an underclass of people chasing affidavits and living at temporary addresses, the first victims of the Nation States. States, the sole victors in any war, were then just beginning to remove their masks and bare their true, tyrannical faces, casting out those of their subjects they no longer wanted, and locking up the rest behind the fences of their borders or inside the stockade of foreign exchange rates.

These stranded individuals did not constitute a population, far less a people; they seemed to be waiting for a train which never came.

My youthful, unacclimatisable impatience grew fretful. I was by birth, temperament and education a Huguenot. Propriety, Decorum, Decency, these three Protestant spirits had attended me since I was in my cradle; I was lacking in social graces and native ease. I had a good chin, but it was square-shaped and my glasses were square-shaped; everything about me was square-shaped, studied, forced; in this easy-going country I felt obliged to follow that synthetic virtue, the supercharged, demanding and no-less square-shaped sense of civic duty which you find in Calvinists, especially at times when moral standards are low. People said of me: "He's not a good mixer, but he's a very organised young man". This I took as a compliment.

Methodical, accustomed to plough my life in straight furrows, I had sketched out a plan of action, with dates, before I left Paris—I would disembark on 3rd November; I'd give myself until 16th December to find a house: then three months to furnish and arrange it to my taste, one month to train up my Arab servants, and all winter to instil a sound routine in the staff working in my office.

Spring should find me ready. I would then assign myself the job of becoming acquainted with a sector (the word came in with Foch) with which I'd had little contact: that of pleasure, all the pleasures—lawful pleasures, it goes without saying. To this end, I should need a partner; I meant a mistress.

These naive calculations were overtaken by the extreme ease with which local life operated. I got it all, very quickly, because none of it was what I really wanted. By 1st January I found myself with house, servants, office, staff, all the elements of my plan. Only the mistress was missing.

II

UNFORTUNATELY, up to this point in my life I had never actually met a woman who suited my taste. I loathed carnal exuberance, the arch of the back, lips pouting like one of Carmen's carnations, cleavages like a dish of hothouse peaches, eyes melting, wide and oversupplied with lashes, swelling rump, bad behaviour passed off as good form, the nonchalance of young women perched on bar stools, wide mouths homing in on the mouths of men.

One of those crises which periodically rock the world had just upset the exchange market. When this brief storm had passed the world of business had relapsed into its usual lethargy and I into my underemployed underactivity. How could I fill my leisure hours? Around me I watched all those Europeans bloom in the easier climate which invariably follows great historical upheavals, replenishing their stock of nervous energy, breathing freely once more. But I didn't know how to breathe. I was bored. I floated in a state of abeyance.

III

I WAS INTRODUCED to Clotilde at a reception given by the Chief Magistrate.

In that kingdom of the vacuous, she seemed at first just another blank; everything about her lacked lustre. She wore a beige suit—simple, perfect. Her movements, so contained, barely initiated, that slightly broken voice, the uncertain colour of her eyes, the delicacy of her physique, all gave her an air of orphaned vulnerability. Women thought her ravishingly beautiful because her looks happened to conform to the current fashion: turned-up nose, eyes like a cat's, head too small for her body, round shoulders, no hips, flat chest, long Merovingian feet, slender arms which did not spoil the line of her jackets, slim thighs which enhanced the hang of her skirts. Few men would have dared think that, made as she was, she was actually rather ugly; but bodily grace does far more for ugly looks than it does for beauty, and Clotilde was grace personified.

Clotilde held out her hand to me (her hands were beautiful, long, slender and supple) and gestured that I was to sit down next to her.

"Do you like it out here?"

The obligatory question, to which I invariably replied with a polite affirmative. A sudden revulsion against formulaic answers made me say, rather brusquely: "No".

"The important thing," Clotilde went on after a moment's silence, "is to take life as it comes."

"Take life as it comes", a hand-me-down phrase which made me cross; but the more I chewed on it the more it acquired a deeper sense.

How do you actually take life as it comes? Could this woman show me? Clotilde lived alone; she was free, she kept her money in my bank and had an absent husband who seemed in no hurry to come home from Siberia, an attaché in a regional outpost, which had suddenly become an embassy of some Russian adventurer who had become the government overnight …

IV

The very next day I called on Clotilde and picked up on the phrase where we'd left it the previous evening:

"Do you 'take life as it comes'? How do you do that exactly?"

"By listening to no one and nothing but myself," she said languidly.

"To your own character?"

"Certainly not. To my mood."

"I understand."

"Do you really? Why must you always want to understand? Why not try guessing, it's much better."

"I'm good at guessing too. I can tell that you're relaxed merely by seeing you in that chair, you don't look at all like someone who's sitting down in it, more like a scarf that's been thrown over the back of it."

"I won't return the compliment. You're sitting on yours as stiff as a poker."

"I've always had teachers for everything, except that. You can be my sitting-down teacher."

Clotilde smiled.

"Lesson one—learn to let go."

V

I LET MYSELF GO with Clotilde. To begin with, I did not really let myself go at all, because the effort to relax merely made me more tense.

What I had to do was to step outside myself, forget self and, to achieve this, I needed to observe Clotilde. I made an effort to watch her more closely: her skin was pale as butter, there were blue blurs on her eyelids and mauve highlights where her temples disappeared beneath the forward sweep of her hair. I also watched her live her life; materially and morally she was free, there was something unpremeditated about her, something uncertain and fragile, which made her infinitely more beautiful.

You felt she was so free that she would be capable even of tossing her freedom away, and take extreme pains in doing it.

She was the absolute opposite of me.

I wanted this affair, just as I had always wanted everything else.

VI

Clotilde had a phenomenal gift for adapting to circumstances. In her ability to assume disguises of all kinds, she invariably seemed to know everything without having to learn the ropes; sensitive and shrewd, whatever turn the conversation took, whatever the nature of the company, she was eternally in tune with the occasion. With her, I should not feel out of my element.

I make a point of reiterating that caprice had no part in my choice. I merely applied the unfussy, selective method I had been taught in the Ministry of Finance.

Never was any equation more clearly stated, never did any man feel freer, more sure of himself.

Never did a fish swim more unerringly into the waiting *madrague* net.

VII

NOTHING IS LEARNT more quickly on the continent of Africa than the art of taking life as it comes. Clotilde taught me not to get exasperated with the time difference in my hours of work, the chaotic nature of a business that never closed day or night, and the organic shambles that is the Orient. The moments I spent stroking her hair, which had the scent and the purple rust of heliotrope, and her fair skin, which did not tan in the sun, grew imperceptibly longer. I went less regularly to my office, where in any case nothing much ever happened. I even arranged to have my dragoman come to Clotilde's house with my letters which I signed supine on a harem ottoman stuffed with compressed straw and covered with yellow damask.

From Clotilde, never a word of reproach or criticism, nor sulky looks or a cross moment, nor an inappropriate question; she never thought that just because she had given herself she had thereby acquired rights over my neckties, my past, my future, my correspondence or my weekends.

The ideal woman, easy to handle, both company and companion, lover and friend, wife and mistress, always free, never a burden, and possessed of the unthreatening indifference and pleasing equanimity of temper which delight the heart of the devout egoist.

VIII

I HAD RESOLVED that once I was settled into my career, I could start 'having fun', as they say with a nudge and a wink, though without knowing exactly what they mean by it. Actually, it comes down to lying in the sun, wearing a carnation in one's buttonhole (something I'd never dared try), and dining in a white dinner jacket, the colour of my innocence. I wanted to go out without a hat, stroll to the office without carrying a leather briefcase, don a suit of close-woven grey cloth, something which in Europe would have struck me as being scandalously raffish. I was the physical equivalent of the class swot, a head that was too big, stuffed too full and perched on narrow shoulders which were underdeveloped in relation to my hips. A man with a large head can do virtually anything, except look elegant. I was determined to take a great deal of exercise to correct my proportions: too late, I was already permanently formed, or rather, deformed. As a reaction, I drank six whiskies a day, rode, ploughed my way amateurishly round the golf course, accepted invitations to fancy-dress parties. Rites of initiation into this petty existence which people call the good life. I longed to exchange good behaviour for good manners. Given my capacity for perseverance, I, who had always finished first in tests and in the top echelon in public examinations, was determined that one day I should get no marks at all for good behaviour.

IX

Love is horribly time-consuming; which is why it flourishes best in the provinces; in Paris, everything puts you in mind of love, women's dresses, the perfumes, the food, the theatres, but no one has time for it there—you only have to look at the novels read by our forefathers, and they knew a thing or two about love—thinking of it, preparing for it, meeting each other, waiting for each other, thinking the same things, living at the same tempo—it filled your whole life. But with Clotilde, everything was much simpler; our love life fed on itself.

We understood each other perfectly without having to speak a word, in the same mysterious way that animals have; to reconstitute our conversations would be more or less impossible, for we remained entombed in interminable silences which were given meaning by looks which lasted as long as our kisses, the pressure of our hands (she had the hot hands of indifference), our caresses. Words are for people who have nothing to say to each other.

X

WE WOULD SPEND the night together, we did it very often, because the nights were an extension of the day, being free of the disruptions of northern countries, by which I mean having to turn the lights on or eating meals at set times. We ate when we felt like it; supine after dinner we would remain looking up at the sky, under the canopy of stars, until the chanting of the mosques turned the town into a single harmonious, murmuring entity, with the call of the muezzin ringing out over every rooftop in the native quarter, while a huge sun leapt up out of the sea. We never went to bed, as decent law-abiding citizens do.

Everything was delight and procured with absurd ease. I had long believed that the relationship between lovers must be a complicated business, that women are dangerous. But here was Clotilde, who answered the phone, never gambled, did not drink, went out only to go to her bank, buy olives or roasted almonds, or have her nails done or her hair permed. She was nothing like the sphinx I had feared so much in my timid adolescent heart. Passive, oriental almost. Nothing delighted me more than to see her return from the market bearing a mass of yellow irises, or an armful of flawless arum lilies which had not been damaged in transit, and her head, like a little girl's, would peep out between calyxes as big as a nun's coif.

When I was at her house, I loved the contrast between her gilt arm-chairs so comfortingly upholstered with scenes from the *Fables* of La Fontaine, her silver plate with its old Paris hallmarks which had come from the recesses of some venerable townhouse in the Marais, and the immense, savage swell of the African hills, flooded with light, which unfurled over us, a sort of sea frozen in time, a kind of terrestrial storm buffeting the last remaining vestiges of some western shipwreck.

Clotilde: an old name which delighted me; it was utterly her just as she herself was like one of the arrows of St Clotilde, all graceful filigree, with the blue of the sky behind showing through.

XI

Hunting, in all seasons, for there was no such thing then as a hunting permit, tuna-fishing at the start of summer, sea-bathing, trips to the souks, with haggling sessions which could last for weeks, riding every morning, mare's tail whisk in hand, for the flies; these occupations formed the settled routine of our lives. We would set off early and be back by the middle part of the day. We'd find our horses waiting for us, barbs which turned skittish the moment you got on them yet were as placid as hobbled mules once you let go of them. We would gallop from *douar* to *douar* along wide trails which in winter get so marshy that we threw up great gouts of mud yet become so hard with the first winds of summer that they seemed to be made of baked clay. The light seeped into the very heart of us; wild flowers rose up and besieged the town—each month brought a new surge of them and simultaneously supplied our guns with a wave of migrating birds:

in February, it was narcissi and lapwing, in March, irises and plover, in April marigolds and quail, in May turtle doves and roses.

The wind blew from east to west and it never stopped; it sprang from its corner throwing right and left hooks, and if calm was momentarily restored, it was inexplicable, accidental—the trees, twisted and bent low, were driven beyond endurance; the ox peckers were blown out of them like magnolia petals; even the storks were swept away lighter than wisps of straw, their large feet dangling; the larks, launched by some invisible spring, hung motionless in the air, wings folded, laughing like silly girls being tickled. The wind was so strong that the stoutest walls creaked like wicker fences and the smoke from chimneys was driven down and flattened against the roofs before it had a chance to write anything on the sky.

XII

WE WALLOWED and rolled in the trough of a depression caused by the confluence of two vast air flows, one oceanic, the other continental. Whenever the wind dropped, we felt light-headed, as if one of the four elements had suddenly gone missing. We surrendered to the daily hurricane which always began with the sun and ended with it.

We had allowed ourselves to be blown along towards our as yet still distant fate, up to our eyes in happiness.

I was dazzled by the freedom of our love-making and the joys of sinfulness. I felt light as a feather. I had never hoped to feel light; it came as a great surprise and gave me intense pleasure. I floated down rivers of milk and honey, dazed by the blueness of the sky, deliquescent in our all-dissolving existence.

XIII

SUCH PERFECT PEACE, in a world in ferment, did not ring entirely true. There were moments when I had a vague sense that someone, or something, was setting a trap for me. "Life is not charitable," I would think, "you can force it to yield scraps of happiness, but if left to itself it will never give you anything."

The sun or moon entering through the slats in the blinds stencilled the wall with braided traceries of gold or silver which seemed somehow too rich, too fine, too uncomfortable for the puritan in me. I stared at them so much that I could stand it no longer and turned my back on them. I had been raised surrounded by the mean-minded wealth, penny-pinching and carefully measured, of god-fearing Protestant circles; things with no price-tag, things that came too easily worried me, I felt I was forever signing cheques which would bounce; I knew that if all you had to do was clap your hands and a tray would appear weighed down with everything you could possibly want, then Satan would be the one carrying it. A premonition? An ancestral survival?

Eventually the last shreds of these northern mists grew threadbare and drifted away. My heart overflowed, my body took its gratifications without a second thought; I gave myself up to a prodigious wonderment, paralysed by the heat as others are by cold.

XIV

It wasn't that Clotilde acquired undue influence over me; on the contrary, she adopted my bootmaker, my decorator, my garage, my brands of drink, my likes and dislikes. I was in the driving seat of our surrey. (Though can you speak of a couple when there is nothing being connected, or of a carriage when there is no common load to carry? Our life was, rather, a free gallop, side by side.) I would sketch out the plan for the day—we would go and buy a Berber ankle bracelet, search out a few antique Fez tureens, yellow, aubergine, green.

We were lovers almost officially; if a tradesman called on one of us and got no answer he would take his goods to the other's house, with that calm composure which makes the manners of the Orient so accommodating. In any case, trying to hide would have been more or less pointless in that small town which was then nothing like the great city where I am kicking my heels today.

XV

IN THOSE DAYS, consulates were still the heart of a residence, centres of political, commercial, legal and social life; each consul went about preceded by his dragoman in his gold-braided uniform who opened a way through the ragged throng with a drum major's staff. The main square, recently renamed Place de la Paix, with its cafés and shoe-shines, concentrated the activity, or rather the inertia, of this Europe in miniature. The Jewish and Portuguese money lenders, who had emerged from the presidios in the country roundabout, had yet to set up in shops of their own; they sat by the roadside to trade and clinked the old Hassani silver coins against the paving stones; the whole street rang with the sound. In the evening the ladies sallied forth mounted on donkeys, preceded by a man carrying a lantern, and every house provided a mounting block at its door for them. In the trees, monkeys played havoc with the first telephone wires. The buildings had mud walls made of sun-baked bricks; reinforced concrete was a thing unknown; only the balconies were made of wood, often driftwood—the lattice covering some windows had been fashioned from the timbers of prows of our Trafalgar ships. Large transactions were settled with bags of silver, in thalers so heavy that oxen were needed to transport them. Flogging was still a local practice, as in the tales of Voltaire; the prison in the kasbah was one of the tourist attractions; visitors went to see the convicts who were held fast by an iron collar riveted to the wall and lived off scraps of charity; the eye could not penetrate the gloom of a chamber with a high-vaulted ceiling supported by pillars which recalled those of the Byzantine baths in Istanbul, and crossed bars, hooped and hammered, where the prisoners, mouths to the ground, devoured the food that was thrown to them. A bar, a bordello and a family boarding-house represented civilisation. No speculator had yet had the idea of buying up dunes which no one wanted. I shot partridge on the spot where, twenty-five years later, my new bank would stand. The only hotel in town was run by a couple from Marseilles whose elderly parents recalled having let rooms to Henri Regnault. In the square, riders still performed those feats of Arab horsemanship so dear to the Romantic painters; at the town gate dervishes beat their foreheads with wooden slats studded with nails and daubed blood all over the bread people gave them.

All that is now gone. On the subject of the growth and development of the town I have begun to offer up lamentations as Jeremiah once did on the laying waste of Jerusalem, which is ludicrous. Such animadversions are on a par with the ramblings of old men which invariably begin 'In those days'; sleek-lined American cars have taken the place of hairy-flanked mules; a forest of babbling radio masts and chattering aerials has sprung up everywhere; today I was served ice cream from a soda-fountain and in my perambulations I have yet to meet the old Negro water-seller with his goatskin and his hair tied up with little brass bells. At my approach, no one has stepped forward to perfume me with the incenses of the harem; I have not seen a single one of those dragomans with belly-dancer eyes and robes of pistachio and salmon who always stood waiting by the flimsy wooden jetty for the skiffs which ferried passengers who had been disembarked far out in the bay and who were still whey-faced from having survived the mortal peril of crossing the bar.

XVI

During the quarter-century which has elapsed between that winter (now grown more distant still by the speeding-up of history) and today, my wounds have healed; they were hideous; I shall try to describe them without inducing disgust in any person who might read these lines. It will have taken the onset of old age and this unscheduled stopover on the edge of Africa to bring me to the point of telling all.

These words will surprise, given that they jar with what I've been saying about the rapt contentment in which I was immersed; indeed, they are so completely the reverse that who would expect to find them at this juncture in the confessions of a man in love?

My closeness to Clotilde, our life, lazy and full of ease, our nearness temple-to-temple, may seem innocent and uncomplicated; in fact, they carried all the dangers of sloth and indolence. The restful attraction of the idea of living together without witnesses, cares or clocks which is evoked by this picture of two human beings with nothing to do and managing their life together very agreeably, is little more than a form of physical comfort and hardly deserves to be called love.

Love it wasn't, not yet; it was merely happiness.

XVII

"WHAT ARE you thinking?"
"Nothing."
"And you?"
"Nothing."

This was the distilled essence of all our conversations, the words most frequently used by lovers everywhere, emblem of the total vacuum in which they coexist. Whenever I try to account for our day-to-day serenity, I never get beyond those two responses which said it all: "Nothing". Our affair was without exuberance of any kind; it was through silence alone that we inhabited each other.

Clotilde would insert the bulge of her shoulder into the hollow of mine and snuggle down, repeating: "Nothing". Her deep waters closed back over that choice word.

The unbroken daydream in which we lived could not have had a better device. "Nothing" translated our ambrosial tedium exactly. "I like being bored," she would say. We savoured boredom because it was not boredom to us. She bought books, perfunctorily, held them open in her lap, but stopped reading on page one if it wasn't about her and her problems; for women, books are just one more mirror. Clotilde looked dreamily at invisible things that hovered above the printed page. The novel she dreamt of rode barebacked on the one in her hand.

" … Nothing … "

XVIII

I WOULD HAVE HAD only one criticism to make of our young lovers, which was that they gave the conventional outward impression of being a highly respectable couple, that they seemed to have one of those unofficial arrangements which pass without comment in great capital cities. It is true that I did set a value on a certain measure of propriety, always indispensable in my view, particularly in small towns; for illicit couples, respectability can be a substitute for virtue—adultery too has its conventions.

I admired in Clotilde her restraint, her levelheadedness, her talent for self-effacement and her reserve which always struck precisely the right note. At tea parties as at the golf club, people thought that she was distinguished, which meant there was nothing particularly distinctive about her. Her self-possession robbed her face of any expressiveness. Perhaps I could have wished her to be more forthcoming; but there, it's not possible to be both passionate and a lady.

Clotilde rarely used the exact words for things. I found the leanness of her physical form repeated in the contours of her mind in which you could detect general threads but few clear-cut lines. Observed on the terrace of her house, instead of being sharply etched against the blue of the sky, her silhouette was somehow blurred. Even her voice was pale, though it faltered very prettily; she was never entirely confident of it, like a singer who tries for the note that is a little too high. None of this excluded a certain remoteness, Clotilde was always in control of herself—if something made her cross, she became exquisitely polite, frighteningly sweet, but over her unfurrowed face would flash a glint of nickel steel.

In times gone by, lovers laid bare their innermost selves with a wealth of nuances of which the theatre and its synthetic but necessary effects preserve one last echo: high-flown language dating from the age of the Romantics enables its heroes and heroines to deliver three lectures about themselves in the space of three acts. But how nowadays could you possibly stage a play featuring modern lovers who live in a world of dreams, half-cooked ideas and tobacco- and alcohol-filled musings, against a background of blaring radio, and exchange monologues which, actually, have a certain nobility of their own. They button their mouths only when it is time for action.

Clotilde gave herself with a natural reserve which flattered my innate crassness and spartan habits.

XIX

OUR COURTEOUS MANNERS did not prevent my mistress from loving me. In any couple, there is invariably one of the two who loves more than the other or, at least, who is the first to love; that one was she. I can say this today without vanity, because it was so.

And because subsequently it was the other way round.

That about-turn was my tragedy.

I adopted a muscular approach to love; just as the Muslims said their prayers morning, noon and eve, so we performed our orisons at the same intervals, and the chant of the muezzin, the only time when the Arab voice is not guttural, when that magnificent call ascends to an unresponsive heaven, frequently served as an accompaniment to our earthly cries. I would fall asleep after our hectic session of physical exercise; once it was over, I never gave it another thought.

XX

I COULD PUT A DATE on the exact moment when my peace of mind began to evaporate. It was the day of the Festival of Sheep.

I was taking a siesta when something or other woke me; I turned my head very carefully, so as not to disturb Clotilde who I thought was lying behind me asleep on her chaise longue.

She was sitting bolt upright, quite motionless and, as it were, out of herself: she wasn't smiling, though she had just smiled, because her mouth was still open and her lips were turned up at the corners, so that her face wore a singular expression; through eyelids like slats in a blind seeped a glint of sea green which I was seeing for the first time. Her irises often changed colour, hazel, slate blue, topaz, but never this strange green. Clotilde's eyes were staring and her nerves were taut, as though she were about to leap up and rush off somewhere.

"What are you thinking?"

She gave a start.

"Nothing."

I felt a weird shiver of foreboding. The expression about feeling someone walking on your grave describes it exactly. I suddenly became aware of the untroubled happiness I had been enjoying at the very moment when something alien crept into it. "Nothing … "

There can be no 'nothing' in love.

Clotilde was keeping something from me, a worry, some secret hurt. I felt anxious; how dear she had become to me, and how necessary!

Slowly, silently, she had taken possession of my life.

XXI

What came next is hard to put into words, for the degrees by which I slid down the slope were barely perceptible.

I had never much bothered myself with Clotilde's thoughts; I imagined they were a reflection of mine; often in passing I caught echoes of my own ideas. Like all women in love, she learnt by osmosis.

I believed I was dealing with a second me.

My simplicity of mind was unbounded.

I had never wondered if Clotilde had had other lovers before me, although the ease of her capitulation should have led me to assume that she had … When I decided to find out more about my mistress, I immediately thought about her husband. Who was he? Did he love her? How had he charmed her? At no point did I put these questions to Clotilde—such a degree of interference would have been unthinkable to me—in matters of love, I was dependable, devoted, direct; never obsessive, curious or nosy; a lover's inquisition was to me the height of crassness.

Which is why, when the need to know had taken hold of me, I made my enquiries elsewhere.

They came to nothing. Around the issue which we have set our hearts on knowing there invariably springs up a tacit conspiracy, in which the biggest fools seem shrewd and the loosest tongues the essence of discretion. I grew discouraged all the more quickly because my natural reserve made it painful for me to ask questions of third parties.

This invisible, remote husband began to haunt me; Clotilde had a way of not speaking of him which amounted to disparagement … Unless, that is, her silence hid regrets which were all the deeper for being unspoken? Perhaps she owed him a great deal, maybe too much? Was it from him that she had acquired her stylish knowledge of the ways of the world? The outsider can be caught on strange thorns when he starts to enquire into the past of two people of whom one is a completely unknown quantity. I was careful and patient; I was determined to assemble the scattered bones with which I would reconstitute the skeleton of a couple that no longer existed.

Chance favoured me. I discovered a jacket overlooked at the back of one of Clotilde's wardrobes. A suit on a hanger looks like a corpse fished out of water. This ghostly garment had clothed a man considerably bigger than me, longer in the leg and built like a prop forward; the slope of the shoulders, the limp hang of the empty, flat sleeves, all hinted at a desperate quest for smartness; the gaping patch pockets suggested slovenliness of mind, a flat contradiction of the attempt at physical chic. I could imagine the body, but how could I come up with a face? I searched the pockets; in one I found an old identity card and a list of things to do.

I shot off to town immediately, bought a book about handwriting and a short introduction to physiognomy. Then, shutting myself away at home, I began examining the evidence I had found. First I studied the writing of the list of tasks and the envelope, addressed to Clotilde and postmarked Vladivostock, on which it had been scribbled. Holding the handwriting book in one hand, I searched eagerly for the direst signs; from the thick down strokes emerged the picture of a violent, dissembling man, cruel and devious: clearly a neurotic, and possibly deranged? And it was this psychopath who had opened the portals of love for Clotilde! Dry-mouthed I scrutinised the feebly-formed letters which were at variance with the sports coat and the athlete's body. I turned eagerly to the photograph on the identity card; it had been taken in the harsh light of a forensics lab and showed the face of a choleric man inflamed by debauchery; a bold nose, heavy mouth, a forehead encroached on by hair at the temples; the eyes of a lynx gleamed out of the faded print which looked as though it had been covered by a blanket of Siberian snow. The whole exuded gross sensuality. Forced by this consummate rake, had Clotilde made discoveries which I had been unable to make her forget?

I had designed my life like a plan on a drawing board. I now vowed that I too would round it out with all the shades of the flesh.

XXII

TRIANGULATING MY PLEASURES, I resolved we should devote one whole week, a week to be spent in cell-like seclusion, to the cultivation of advanced sexuality. The sport of the poor, sex now became our drug distilled by solitude and sloth, the only form of escape available to the two of us who were prisoners of my vow of confinement. 'Living love's young dream'—the expression haunted me; in my mind I could hear an exquisite sound, which began piano and swelled to forte, as if plucked from a string of gold and silk stretched to breaking point. I was going to have to pursue my exploration of our coupling to the same exquisite pitch. What I had in mind was a kind of splendid tournament, with a divan to serve as lists, where in isolation, by even and sustained stages, I should succeed in taking our feelings to the level of ecstasy.

Clotilde to be sure was happy. When she felt my rapture burst in her, her hand took mine tenderly and squeezed it; it was as though she were a chit of a girl, curious and awkward, whose senses are still to be awakened who and allows you to initiate her into the games of love.

Happy, yes, but not blissfully so. I gave her what ministers of religion, when they advise the newly married, call 'the satisfactions to which a woman is entitled'. Could I say that she remained frigid in my arms? Her burning cheeks, moist lips, her responses to my biddings all gainsaid it. And yet ...

XXIII

THE FATMA WOULD LEAVE our dinner trays outside. The postman slipped the mail from my bank under the door. The phone stayed off the hook. We never got out of bed, lathered in our own odour which coated our skins like toad spittle. We knew each other's bodies by heart; in the dark, we ran our hands over their every detail, the way the blind read Braille. Our sheets were heavy with the carbon dioxide we exhaled; the only air I breathed in was the air which Clotilde breathed out; she still had the delectable breath of the very young.

My head was in a whirl, meanwhile day followed night, though we paid it no heed. The days went by in a blur, just as in those old films where the wind blows away the leaves of a calendar. Such divisions of time had ceased to have any meaning for us; we had substituted a rhythm of our own.

I have only vague memories of those days spent in willing seclusion, but there is one, very vivid, of the dazzling brightness reflected by the terrace which shone directly into my oversensitive eyes. Semi-darkness, then darkness, then suns in orange and green skies—to which we bade farewell in the west only to find them reappear in the east—were replaced by stars, the stabbing beams of the lighthouse, and a huge moon which wore the authentic face of a hanged man.

Sometimes clouds, maybe a storm, would serve to batter our nerves raw. In the bitter hour which follows the expenditure of sexual energy, I ached all over, in my back, obviously, in the nape of my neck, in my muscles. Every part of me, irritated with so much chafing, swollen, tumescent, became the seat of a new pain. Our bed sheets were smudged with the black of our cigarette ash, carmined with lipstick, stained with the yellow of our breakfast eggs, sticky with marmalade.

Tightly intertwined, we stayed like plaited willow branches for the whole of that week which was as long as a century. And braided together we remained, incapable of getting up, of separating, of letting go of each other, we had become Venus flytraps, bloodsuckers, microscopic infusoria endowed with only primitive consciousness. Our organisms functioned only by habit. We no longer performed actions; our actions performed themselves. Touch was no less painful than the other senses; the lightest caress now made us clench our teeth. Wild physical desire no longer rose up boiling out of our exhausted state; what remained now was a kind of grim, mulish perseverance, lucid or unfocused by turns as we alternated between rapture and nausea, which produced no more than an athletic response. I needed to know what lay beyond mere physical possession. But our awareness grew dimmer and whatever lay beyond it continued to retreat before us.

Fatigue led merely to an all-encompassing haziness which resembled the dark night of the mystics, and to separation from Clotilde, which was infinitely more painful than if she had refused to give herself from the outset.

XXIV

CLOTILDE'S EYELIDS had turned blue. She was thinner; lying down plus the absence of exercise had robbed her of the meretricious benefit of the upright position, the artificial posture of social life, and gave her the look of an animal curled up in a ball of anxious torpor which accentuated her air of remoteness.

She was becoming more animal than woman.

For an age, for hours, we had stopped wanting each other. So why did we stay in bed like that? Such an idiotic marathon! Nothing made sense any more; the lamp stayed lit though it was day. The days turned torrid and we would have been far better off on the beach. We had moved beyond the stage of satisfaction, even of satiety.

I feigned a level of well-being I no longer felt. Ashamed to say outright that lying in bed had gone on far too long for me, that I'd had enough of having my face licked not washed, I now yearned for the open sea, for clean water, so that I might be rid of the sticky plankton in which we were marinating.

XXV

WHY DID I REMAIN as I was without ever making myself get out of bed? I would not have been able to give any intelligible reason. I sensed there was a kind of mental gulf between Clotilde and me which I could not bridge. All those oh-so-busy hours which as they accumulated should have brought us closer seemed only to drive us apart. Though I lay on top of her (deceptively thin women make the best air beds) and held her so close that no daylight showed between the hollow recesses of our bodies, I felt her become increasingly distant. I grew in invention, I devised new amorous arts, but failed to extract from her anything more than short-lived spasms.

There were occasions when she stared at me with those speckled eyes of hers which would turn suddenly black. Bright flecks floated up in them like bubbles in glasses of champagne lit by the light of candelabras. It seemed she was about to say something. Then the moment would pass. The effort she made to hold back the words made her mouth smaller. There was no room for two on the road on which she had set her foot.

Anyone seeing her at that time would have said she was completely fulfilled. The condescending view I had of her reassured me. I prided myself on having been kind, not yet having learnt that lovers are never kind. But as I watched her, a Clotilde who seemed defeated, defoliated, her arms bruised by my lips, as soft as the pillow on which she lay her superfluous beauty, gazed at me with upturned eyes which she had not the strength to open wide but were not the eyes I wished to see in her face.

XXVI

I WAS A MERE BEGINNER, though not to the extent that I did not know the difference between a woman who allows herself to be taken and a woman who gives herself. Clotilde gave herself; I recognised that moan, a faint whimper barely more audible than those which had gone before, which was the last; it passed her lips almost reluctantly and she would collect herself at once, blushing from what I took to be a chaste pleasure.

Now, a man who knew women better would not have been misled; he would have seen the mouth crowded with stifled groans, the eyes puffy with repressed tears; as for the neck, still swollen, lips weary but still hungry and chewing on each other, he would have soon guessed that Clotilde was drowning. He would have felt her nipples always hard against him; he would have noted the heave of her pelvis, insidious, unconscious (if it hadn't been she would have stopped it); he would have understood the meaning of her expression—uncertain, expectant.

I did not know that the sheets of a bed make an iron cage in which one fighting insect must devour the other, according a form of guerrilla warfare in which neither mercy nor quarter is given, full of surprises, of foul play, where the complexion of the hostilities changes hourly, in short I was unaware that there is nothing less natural than the primal act of nature, for through it reality breaks in upon the dream of love and upon the idea of sex that lies in the brain, its controlling master.

I was as yet acquainted only with the smiling face of love—I was about to see it scowl.

XXVII

One night when there was a moon, I was aware of something gently but insistently brushing against the entire length of my body, and of an accompanying rapid muttering.

Clotilde fidgeted a great deal as she slept and sometimes she talked in her dreams; I was used to it and the restlessness of her sleep had ceased to disturb mine; but of late everything my consort did put me on a state of alert. Instead of nudging her to shake her out of her nightmare, I pretended to be asleep and gently edged my head nearer until it nestled against hers, so that I was best placed to hear the celestial reverberation of that miniature organ that is the human larynx.

The sense of what she was saying escaped me at first: the words ran together in brief snatches, also incomprehensible; then the half-phrases joined up to form a monologue that took my breath away. Clotilde's legs came together tightly, in the manner of the women who operate sewing machines and are so excited by the rhythm of the treadle that their cheeks flush red then suddenly lose their colour ... Eyes glazed, she played with her body from which, with savage fury and the tips of her finger-nails, she extracted strident, sustained moans. And all the while she clung to me; and yet she asked nothing of me; it was as if she needed some crumb of human contact, of human warmth (but would not an animal have served the purpose as well?) before she could be set moving. I was the frontier of flesh across which she fled to another country, leaving me numb and bereft. She looked at me with sightless eyes, as invalids do who have turned in on themselves and refuse to acknowledge the world around them.

She was enacting an invisible drama, there, pressed hard against me.

I whispered softly:

"Clotilde, what are you doing?"

"Telling myself things."

"What things?"

"Mad things."

"Tell them to me."

"No."

I had stopped being an object of pleasure for her. But then, had I ever been?

That week of exhausting sequestration, far from delivering her to me, swept her up into a dark world in which she began to feel a desire that had no end and ran counter to mine.

Then suddenly Clotilde stopped talking, limp, mouth open as if on the point of death, eyes such as I had never seen before.

This unexpected sight of a stranger in a trance of rapture, jettisoning a heart altered beyond recognition, left me feeling shattered. My mistress had been absorbed into a world crammed with thoughts that goaded her with the whip of a pleasure beside which whatever I could offer her was but a feeble copy. Thoughts so vile in their grotesque unfolding that I cannot set them down here …

XXVIII

At first light I got out of bed, rushed out and plunged into the sea, swam for an hour, then went back to my office.

There I collapsed into an armchair and fell into an exhausted sleep.

When I woke, I had the feeling I must have dreamt if not all, then at least most of what had happened that night. I was pretty hard on myself; my unforgivable experimentation had upset Clotilde's nerves; it was enough to drive her mad. It was vital I put an end to my reprehensible meddling, I must try to forget it all, get back to normal life.

Actually, our life did start up again, with its long evenings of intimacy and healthy forms of relaxation. The edges of the crevasse had closed over what I sincerely hoped had been an ephemeral dream. I told myself that the communion of our two souls had not ended … But in my heart of hearts, I was only partly taken in. In one moonlit night, I had learnt that Clotilde was not uncomplicated nor charming nor temperate—that she was not what I thought.

A lengthy interval elapsed without anything happening to ruffle the surface. The rift had been mended.

Our times alone captured all the monotony of a sea crossing. The terrace, which might have been a pasteboard set, where we spent the evenings, the outlines of the studio window, razor-sharp against an adamantine sky and barely attenuated by a white-and-green-striped awning, made the authentic bridge of a liner. To complete the illusion, the *fatma* would wheel out a trolley loaded with little delicacies better suited to stimulating the appetite that to satisfying it. I would not have thought it out of the way if someone had come up to me and said: "Have a splendid crossing, sir."

XXIX

WE WENT TO THE CINEMA quite often. In small towns and in the colonies, films are becoming a necessary drug. The perfidious screen, for all its semblance of blank neutrality, is a wholesale liberator of the motions of the spirit which are repressed by caution and fear. The silent films of those days generated a magic which did not survive the advent of the talkies.

I can see the auditorium now, so different from the present-day American-Arab palaces. It was a kind of long trench with walls washed a yellowish colour, plastered with bright posters of westerns, packed with burnouses, stray dogs wandering among the rows of seats and donkeys parked at the ticket office; the ceiling was open like the roof of a car and through the gap millions of stars looked down on their sisters, the stars on the silver screen.

It was at the far end of this squalid pit that one evening Jackie Coogan materialised, freckle-faced, and with his cap pulled down over his ears. He was a double revelation: of the childhood of an art and of the art of childhood.

On another evening, I took Clotilde to see a film which showed scenes set in an orphanage; kids came pouring out through a door like a torrent from a mountain gorge; legs stick-like above the concertinaed socks which spilt over their clumping shoes. I admired their sly eyes, the obscene faces they pulled, the tongues they poked out: such prepubescent squalor, a heaving mass of cruel animals and toadying sucking-up.

For some moments I had been aware of a tingling, the sort you get from an electric cable, all down one arm; I didn't give it a second thought until a more insistent tremor spread to my whole body. In the dark I couldn't make out Clotilde's face very clearly; suddenly I had the impression that it was different, in some way coarsened; all that was sylphlike and graceful had been wiped off it; I saw a profile that was sharp, riveted on the screen, a head held high, aggressive, ophidian, with a bold chin beneath a mouth that was ready to bite, bite anything: Clotilde, a hunting animal ready to pounce on its prey.

What enslaving power was the film exerting over her? What fanciful images, idyllic or barbarous, what garish pictures was she projecting onto that screen where I saw only scenes of innocence? I should have shaken her out of her trance and dragged her away, but I sat there stunned, watching a film in which I could see nothing in the least capable of bringing on an orgasm, and I remained where I was, rubbing shoulders with her inconceivable abandon.

With one hand on her lips, Clotilde seemed barely able to stifle a sound like a pigeon's cooing; suddenly, as if struck down, she gave a shriek which made the people in the seats near us turn their heads.

I stood up at once; ashamed of her shriek, Clotilde clung to my arm and allowed me to take her outside.

XXX

I SHOULD HAVE forced matters that same evening and extracted an explanation. But the life of the senses cannot be explained any more than the unconscious in which it has its roots. Perhaps Clotilde, who dreamt with her eyes open, had forgotten her orgiastic whoop.

What rope could I use to climb down to reach the bottom of her silence?

And once I got there, what would I do? What was I to do with Clotilde?

I was afraid of her and very likely of myself. I had the impression of escorting to her door a woman I did not know; my ineptness returned in strength; I did not feel I was clever enough to undertake the reclamation of someone whose mind was depraved. When confronted by such refined sensuality, I also felt somewhat hampered by my own immature sexuality, by my approach to love-making which was so crude when set beside what was quite possibly a work of art, where inspiration could lead to something miraculous.

I opted to do what seemed the easiest course: I said nothing.

And yet my need to understand a human being who was so close to me, to possess her secret, left me no peace. I felt impelled to explore the images with which she was deceiving me as surely as if they had been another man.

XXXI

But were they just images? Did not her phantasms have human faces? Dreams of love, like all other kinds of dreams, have their beginnings in reality. How could a young woman who goes out and about by herself, rides alone, walks unescorted through the Arab quarters, have only the warped inclinations of some pert miss who is a pathological liar, or the lubricious visions of a hallucinating hermit? Surely her raging lust had to have its roots in something real which existed or had once existed? 'These things you can't make up', as they say.

I took a decision—I would keep a close watch on Clotilde.

XXXII

At first I did nothing of the sort. I had no stomach for the role of policeman; at least that was the excuse I gave my pusillanimous impulse to turn a blind eye and remain in the dark. Why could I not just settle for living with both Clotildes, the one who lived in my world and the other who gazed down into an abyss of foulness and dreamt of pleasure? The imagination is another planet; I would abandon it to her. Was it not preferable that, driven by her senses, she should turn narcissistic rather than promiscuous? Did I not possess the better part of her? Surely this whole business was on a par with that groundswell of dark desire which allows slightly jaded, decent, middle-class marriages to mend themselves? When there is a mad woman in the attic, does it not matter less that she is mad than that she stays in the house?

XXXIII

WE WENT ON LIVING the same insular existence and our two hearts continued to be joined on the same agreeable footing. I had the feeling that, by a curious compensating effect, the smaller the role I had in her physical life, the larger the place I occupied in her feelings. Vehemently and on every possible occasion, Clotilde gave me demonstrations of her affection and regard for me, as if to say that sex and love for her were mutually exclusive worlds. In any case, even if Clotilde heavily favoured her closet urges, her secret lust was a tyrant which never sought to conspire against me nor did it prevent me from enjoying my precious pleasures. Clotilde went on being the refined creature, always open to all that is elevated, fine and moving whom I had known and chosen. And even amid the delicious tractations of the flesh, I could honestly say that I had not stopped pleasing her.

XXXIV

But exactly how much did I please her?

Being constitutionally incapable of sensing these things, I had no choice but to wait before I could understand. What I did now begin to understand, in fits and starts, was that trying to possess another through the flesh is the equivalent of trying to stab a ghost. When I took Clotilde, she was happy, she was delighted, but she was not satisfied. I had thought that she was not highly sexed. Men do not believe many women are. It is the cause of much unhappiness. Women are all highly sexed, it's just that for most of the time the spring that releases the mechanism remains undiscovered. It would appear that nature intended there to be a singular lack of consonance between the sexes, between our urgent need for gratification and their often interminable procrastination; this being particularly true in cases involving women who, like Clotilde, have the fiercest appetites. She was simply asking her phantoms to supply what she had ceased to expect from me.

I could be part of her liberation, but I was not her liberator.

XXXV

Then it all started up again. The devil was at the bottom of it, as with those Italian tureens where his grinning face appears once all the diners have been served.

For us Protestants, confession has all the attraction of forbidden fruit. Accordingly I did not try to stop her lips, those delta-like lips through which a muddy river flowed.

Where, when, to whom, to what did Clotilde give herself? She always spoke in the past tense, it was often a past that was recent but impossible to check and it slipped through my fingers.

At that time, the value of our currency was plummeting. This meant many unforeseen hours of work for me. When I had to be away, on a business trip or doing the local rounds, Clotilde would always begin by saying that nothing at all had happened during my absence.

But come the night, from her own lips, I learnt that she had put her solitude to an all too profitable use.

This toing and froing between doubt and certainty was making me ill; I was off balance, I chased shadows, I stumbled over the naked body which blocked the threshold of truth ... Clotilde had all day to relax whereas I had to work, glued to the phone, rushing from one bank to the next with obsession following hard on my heels. I no longer did anything well, all I thought of was how I could wring the necks of her incubi. What Thales remarked to the elusive Proteus I could have said to Clotilde: "I know you are not speaking to me from the place where you are."

Even if Clotilde did not actually do all the things she was capable of, was that not still serious too? To desire is to act and the edifice Clotilde was constructing was collapsing around my ears whether or not she had built it in her imagination or with real acts of vileness.

Master of myself, master of the two of us, this I still was, to outward appearances. I did not see that I was in the process of losing that authority. I allowed Clotilde to acquire the kind of influence over me which was like that wielded over an old man by a perversely-inclined girl.

Night is the realm of woman; our nights cast long shadows over my waking days. The perilous depths into which my mistress was venturing began to exert their spell on me.

XXXVI

The odious thrill of relief I felt the moment she was no longer in my arms deserved to be consigned to immediate oblivion, but now it asserted itself in my mind. I thought about it all the time.

I felt despair to see someone I loved sinking into such depravity; although its centre was most likely located outside consciousness, it was nevertheless an appalling form of moral degeneracy. I have said that my childhood was in no way impure; for all the fondlings, dreams, friendships, chance encounters, newspapers, photographs, in short all the paraphernalia which attend the eroticism of our adolescent years, none of my nerve centres had been tainted. It was my healthy temperament that made my gorge rise. Shame and anguish vanquished anger; the idea of loving and continuing to love a woman for whom normal carnal relations have become something unnatural filled me with gloom and disgust.

XXXVII

But I was beginning to need that disgust more and more.

XXXVIII

I WENT ON FEELING exactly the same way about her body, as passive as a discarded burden, in which each night I spent the essence of my youth and vigour. I went in search less of pleasure than of the permanently elusive reassurance that I was able to please Clotilde every whit as much as the images which were usurping my place; I was also seeking the illusion that ultimately I could defeat them, that in the end I would be loved only for myself if only I worked at it for long enough.

XXXIX

What should I have made of it all? An aberration of the senses, or of the mind? Was she lying? Had she really done all the things she admitted to when her soul split and cracked? Was the violation of childhood she boasted of an authentic memory of lived experience or a fiction spawned on the far side of her consciousness?

I took the horns of my dilemma and shook them like the iron bars of a prison.

XL

I HAD HOPED that her mysterious perversion would gradually fade with time. But the very opposite occurred. Not only did it turn into a ritual, but the fever in Clotilde's brain started to spread to mine. I found in that ignoble creature an attraction that was not to be resisted. The tension, intermittent but persistent and recurring which lay hidden beneath both the quiescence demanded by social convention and the ordered routine of the rest of my existence which was spent in the company of a perfectly unmysterious being, plus the animal instincts lurking in the wings of the plain life of a lady golfer, combined to suck me in like an incantation. How could someone of such civilised instincts sail upon such waters of iniquity?

XLI

I HAD OCCASIONALLY TRIED to make light of it all, to treat it as a figment of the imagination, or at most as silly nonsense; and also to come up with some medical explanation for it—' ... Stimulus required for the proper functioning of the medullary reflexes ... '

But it only took the sight of Clotilde cooing and panting, lost in another world, her entire body thrashing, head tossing and turning, hips thrusting as if on springs, a Clotilde in my arms possessed by something that was not me, to leave me completely nonplussed. Every night I was vanquished by a bacchante who lived only for the moment when she had no one to please but herself.

When our interlocked bodies finally untwined and I got out of bed, not only was I physically drained but my mental armour was shattered. Clotilde was lethal.

XLII

Such close proximity to unfettered passion began to have, on the man of settled habits that I was, curious effects. I experienced the first dread stirrings of those selfsame abominable instincts. I could not detach myself from the primitive creature who waited each night for the civilised woman to leave the field to her.

I dared not risk asking questions (I was too afraid that one clumsy move on my part would silence Clotilde altogether). But the rate of her disclosures accelerated. Her madness no longer emerged in the occasional outburst, as on that evening at the cinema; I now observed it resurface continually. I felt shame for her who talked, and for myself who said nothing. I suffered agonies when I felt her under me, constrained, stickily clinging. I could not bring myself to believe she had taken part in such horrible revels, although they had the ring of truth. The more I suffered, the more I was driven to add to my suffering, my very pleasurable suffering. As I leant over her it was now I who seemed to be asking this of her. I waited anxiously for the bricked-up window to be unbricked, for her eyeballs to start swinging wildly like the pointers of a demented compass, waited until Clotilde's bogus voice, her daytime voice, the one she used to declare no trumps or to comment on a golf handicap, was replaced by that other, rough-edged voice. My imagination was not yet ready to be ignited by the blaze of her flaming perversity—it was far too weird—but I was becoming more and more curious about her museum of horrors.

Her secret life eventually sucked me in, turned me into a *detective* not because it was life but because it was secret.

XLIII

Having hesitated for some time about whether I should make Clotilde keep her mouth shut, I finally decided to force her to talk. She regularly dodged my questions, but when she could no longer contain herself the flood of details which she uncorked, hardly pausing to take breath, her instant responses to my sharpest questions were enough to convince me that I was not dealing with a hoaxer.

"I had them on the beach … "

"Who are you talking about?"

"Delicious children, as pretty as night … I held them by the hand and took them round the back of a bathing hut … Could anyone see us? No. We were hidden by the dune. Really? There aren't any dunes just there? More than likely we never went that far when we've been out riding! You remember the mouth of that wadi … "

What she said, beside which the romps of Tiberius

or Krupp on the isle of Capri paled into insignificance, suddenly acquired the extraordinary feel of fact.

Like a sleepwalker, Clotilde obeyed her own radar, never hesitating. I went with her, feeling my way in the dark, wondering if she were walking on the moon, if I were party to some warped invention, or if what I was hearing was after all a genuine confession.

But yes—she had indeed done everything she said she had.

This Clotilde, stripped bare, terrifying, as selfish and as consumed by appetite as the other was temperate and malleable, now dominated me. Meekly, almost eagerly, I followed her into her shadowy sanctuary where she offered up incense to fantastic gods. I was now ashamed to make love straightforwardly, ashamed of my modest but hoggish and even voracious sexual regimen which was a joyless thing when set beside her orgiastic quest.

XLIV

THE MISTRESS with whom I galloped each noon along the beach beneath the hovering wings of stationary sparrow-hawks and through the storks as they glided down to land, she, the sweet companion of my days, had begun, I noticed, to change, as I had. This was strongly brought home to me one morning by the way she handed me my cup of coffee, in the manner of her approach, a thin, absent smile on her face and head lowered like a goat about to charge.

She was not the same person. She had retreated into a stubborn silence. I had never seen her with that grim-set jaw, the lines that ran down in deep grooves from the base of her nose, the eyebrows arched as though astonished by the secret thoughts which they screened from the world. She seemed to be asleep on her feet, her eyes sightless.

All day, she walked through the streets, around her apartment, in the garden of the large Arab house I had rented on the cliff top to which she came most days, wearing a peculiar expression on her face, as if she were inwardly sneering. Nor did she stop smiling like a mad thing, a beatific smile; at table, she would keep her eyes on her plate and all I saw of her was the top of her head. Her sly laughter exasperated me; it was as if, for her own exclusive amusement, she were telling herself some very good jokes indeed.

XLV

Then finally the night came when she spoke a name:
"Ibrahim ... you are black, like a devil ... and you melt in the mouth ... "

Ibrahim! Now I had something tangible to hold on to, something real, not just a groan extracted by the incubus but a clear admission that she had a confederate in her debauches, a man of flesh and blood. Who was he? "I'll find out," I vowed, "I'll find him!"

But I did not proceed immediately to implement the decision I had taken to end the ambiguity once and for all; was this attributable to an inhibition prompted by an unconscious desire to live with doubts which encourage the microbes which consumed me and would have been destroyed by a burst of certainty? I could not bring myself to make a start on my enquiries.

XLVI

Turning up unexpectedly at Clotilde's one morning, I found her in the kitchen busy doing the woolly hair of a small Berber girl, trying with rapt concentration to comb it up.

Standing at her side was a little boy whose Moorish features were already too precociously set for a ten-year-old; he was staring at her, never blinking, with eyes of white enamel.

"That's Ibrahim, and this is his sister, Haïcha," said Clotilde, with disingenuous calm.

"Ibrahim!" I said, taken aback.

("Him, Ibrahim? Absurd!" I thought. "But there, they're all called Ibrahim in this country … ")

"That's right, Ibrahim and Haïcha … " repeated Clotilde through her painted lips, stretching her mouth into the shape of a heart, her daytime mouth, the mouth all women have. (At night she had her own, her real mouth, uncrimsoned, which disturbed me in quite a different way.)

The little boy's skull was clean shaven and looked like a blue pebble. The girl presented Clotilde's exquisite hands with a matted thatch under which the nape of her neck showed greyish mauve.

The child had such natural elegance, shoulders held well back, elbows close to her sides, back emphatically arched ... She hadn't even given me a second glance, for she was gazing fascinated at the gold chain around Clotilde's wrist.

"They've come a very long way; they both rode on a donkey not as big as them. They leave their *douar* when it is still dark with wild asparagus to sell, so they can be at the market by daybreak."

"But how long have you known them?"

"Months."

The Clotilde who answered, while she went on untangling the girl's hair, was she of the grey-gold eyes, the Clotilde of old, charming and elegant.

In her wide-pleated white dress, she shimmered with purity, and the two swarthy children she had around her were like a couple of flies on icing sugar. It all look utterly natural and perfectly proper. I searched in vain for signs of a secret collusion between them. Dissembling came so easily ...

Or could it be that Clotilde was really just playing with dolls?

One night's disclosures would tell me which.

"*Cigarro?*" the boy said in a beggar's whine the moment he noticed me.

Clotilde's pretty fingers went on combing the girl's thatch; they did their level best to shape it into a tuft, like a little lark.

"It would do more good if you deloused her," I said.

XLVII

It all made an attractively innocent picture which set my mind at rest. But not for long. My over-punctilious nature compelled me to examine my conscience and a new source of torment emerged. Was I not as guilty as Clotilde of the vice of Imagination? For had I not allowed it to become a habit?

Could I not be accused of complicity … ?

Absolutely not. I was simply not up to competing with Clotilde in the lechery stakes and, if left to myself, quite incapable of reading the runes of the startling revelations which proceeded from her unpainted mouth. But she was more than capable of supplying me, unaided, with the depraved nourishment I was beginning to find suited my taste all too well: though I did not yet admit it, I was gradually being infected by the contagion of her cerebral lusts. I would look forward to the time when I should press an eager ear against that door of secrets. I now needed the closeness of the limpet embrace of a mistress rich in fabrications and dark fancies.

I still thought that what I felt for her was nothing other than fine and good, that I had already reached the level of her animal soul, to the deciphering of which I devoted myself exclusively and which I likened to the bodies of those fabled beasts made of disparate body parts, a vulture's beak with the spindly legs of a crane, the head of a lion with a dragon's tail.

And so, in the person of Clotilde, 'the graciousness of the mistress of the house', 'the charm of the lady who dines out' were fabulously coupled with the persistence of a bawd and the wanton abandon of a maenad.

XLVIII

Nowadays you often hear it said that human feelings are uncommunicable dreams travelling along tracks which may run in parallel or deviate but never converge. In our case it was the opposite; I communed with Clotilde, I loved her most of all in those fantasies where I could at last merge with her.

Reality or fiction? Unsure of which to choose, I lurched from one extreme to the other, my mind turn by turn made up and uncertain; convinced at times that I was living inside the delusions of a mad woman scorched by the flame of crazy visions which she had devised entirely out of her own head; at others, quite sure I was dealing with an unambiguously cynical woman of debauched propensities.

These contradictory certainties alternated in my mind.

Why could I not see into the heart of this darkness with eyes as cold, as dead, as indifferent as those of Clotilde's husband in that small photograph?

Why can't we kill thoughts the way we kill people, with a gun?

I felt I was going mad.

Mad with love, too. Crippled by love. I shut my mind to all other thoughts. All my conscientiousness, all the fastidiousness of my mind devoted now, not to my work but to my passion, had the awful effect of exacerbating it: utterly obsessed with myself, I sank to brutish depths, to the level where mortal creatures are beyond redemption. I would suddenly start weeping as old men do, shedding heart-wrenching tears, not only of vexation but of anger, for there was nothing I could do to stop them. Who could I talk to? A soul in torment can unburden itself, but where is the sympathetic ear that vice can turn to? The warped and twisted may be allies; they can never be comforters.

And so I went round and round in circles, trapped in a labyrinth of misery and love.

XLIX

THREE-PERSONED HECATE, queen of the night, ate dogs for her sustenance; like the dread goddess, Clotilde ate puppies, I mean the children she made her fodder.

No brave heart she, yet a-hunting she would go, and with unimaginable boldness, venturing even into the most populous areas of the town. She would return bearing small bodies traded to satisfy her unholy desires and then, raising her hand to them, forcing them into terrified submission, proceed to make them perform acts which must surely have surpassed even the foulest practices of the Orient, where precocious childhood is propelled unceremoniously into the halls of vice.

L

I GAVE MYSELF, in clarion tones, positive assurances that I was horrified, but I had gone well beyond the stage of horror, and the pleasure she took in her black and monstrous saturnalia became necessary to mine. The daytime Clotilde, serene of face, now left me unmoved; it was the other, wild, keening Clotilde who made me feel faint with ecstasy and was now my idol.

An idol of clay.

LI

ONE NIGHT, the old Clotilde reappeared, the Clotilde who did not speak, who confessed to nothing, the Clotilde *of the old days*; beautiful and willing, stepping out of her bathrobe like a statue off its pedestal.

I was appalled to find myself admitting that she left me cold. I ran my hands over her body as though it were one of Canova's blue marbles which broadcast their multiple charms in vain, for to the senses they communicate only their chill.

Under my smoothing hands, Clotilde grew excited. I pushed her away with a degree of irritation which matched the unquiet passion which consumed me.

LII

THAT TIME WAS, in its brevity, the most decisive period of my life. To it I applied the pedantic, methodical approach I bring to everything I do. I cultivated evil, the way consistory courts cultivate virtue. I threw myself into goatishness with all the deliberation of purpose which had presided over the whole of my career.

LIII

THE LINES OF ENQUIRY I followed led me from town to country, from the kasbah to the *douars*. Here and there I picked up Clotilde's tracks but always too late—the speed at which she moved was phenomenal. Wherever I went I discovered she had slipped away; she was nowhere. I would come across her little yellow motor car, always empty. One day I would swelter through the busy crowd in the fish market, my feet sunk in ooze, and emerge covered in sardine scales; the next, I would be out on country trails, eating the dust of straggling lines of Berber women who, faces unveiled and heads covered with huge straw hats held on by twists of black wool, walked bent under a load of charcoal or were engulfed by straw mats woven in their village from the bottom of which their calloused feet peeped out under leather gaiters. Sometimes beneath the town's verdant walls, I scoured the coves where foxy young boys lay in wait among the rocks for whatever might come along; at other moments, moving inland, on the crest of a hill topped by the square block of some Muslim shrine, or on the floor of a valley ringing with the raucous cries of ploughmen swearing at their oxen, I would be chased ferociously by beige and white dogs with fur bristling like hyenas. Between the two slopes covered with dark eucalyptus trees, the sea-capped town stacked its tiered huddle of pink and beige walls and white terraces; fields of green corn, of beans the colour of excavated bronze artefacts and, where the soil was newly turned, pools of black ringed by irises; I walked through fallow fields where stalks of dead maize crackled under my feet. The hills unfurled in gentle waves or rocky plateaus and on their tops I could see the shapes of watchful shepherds, backs to the wind, well wrapped up, vainly trying to wrestle their ancient folds from the snatching breeze. I took up with poachers, men who hunted with slings, men who robbed nests and kept live hen-birds in their hoods. I played hop and skip with small boys who herded their black, white-saddled lambs by throwing stones at them. I spoke a Spanish dialect laced with Arabic.

"Have you seen the blonde lady who often rides out this way?"

I ran up against the blank faces of some, the suspicious malice of others who self-servingly said yes and held out their hands. It was as if the little savages, so precocious that they seemed to have been born pubescent, saw clean through me.

In the fallow maize fields, I roamed among men keeping an eye open for the crests of birds. Dressed in mud-coloured rags, they crouched against the easterly wind and acted as caretakers to these backwater villages, for no quarter of the horizon escaped their vigilance. I lived in the company of the small girls who tended those absurd African animals which have a large cow's head stuck on the body of a goat. Escorted by urchins who swarmed around me at knee level, I investigated the walls of cactus which protect villages and are used for drying washing on.

"Tell me if you've seen … "

"*Cigarro!*" (They could blast me with a lungful of garlic at ten paces).

In the market I spotted Ibrahim's blue skull among the crowd of boy porters who, their stick legs entangled in their huge provision baskets, waited outside the white door in horseshoe formation for the European housewives to emerge.

"Is Madame in the souk?" I asked, peering intently into the liquid depths of his eyes.

"*Si … si …* "

"She's not in the souk?"

"*No … no …* "

He answered no, Arab style, tossing his head back and clicking his tongue against his soft palate, exuding slyness. I could have clipped him round the ear for those alternating 'yes's and 'no's. Fear or politeness, Oriental style.

I could be seen waiting outside the Jewish academy, the Spanish school when classes resumed, the Anglican college at daily assemblies, and meanwhile the bell for break at the Lycée Gambetta became a familiar sound to me.

I was making a fool of myself and wasting my time.

LIV

NOT FAR FROM WHERE I LIVED, among the bamboo groves, was a native school which overlooked the road that wound up to the top of the hill. It was just a hut; through the door, which was always open, floated the delightful murmur, as of a swarm of bees, of a Muslim prayer being recited aloud. I had parked my car outside the school. I could see the children squatting on straw mats, their slates hanging round their necks; we exchanged looks.

At night Clotilde often babbled about a school, about her pickings when classes were over.

It had to be this one. These were the same bamboo groves of the small patch of jungle where she had confessed to having taken her less than innocent pleasures.

Propelled into the street by an unseen oriental slipper, a small urchin in baggy, torn trousers fetched up against me. He was crying. I told him to get in the car and tried to cheer him up, so that he wouldn't be so upset about being sent out of class. His tears mingled with snot; he leaked comprehensively. I also told a little girl to get in; she had a star tattooed on her forehead and, in her electric-blue silk robe, was dressed with all the cheap splendour of poor Arab children. Their muddy feet made marks on my upholstery. I gave them Turkish delight and did my best to get them to talk. I tried to imagine how excited Clotilde must have felt at being at such close range to these young animals with their firm, supple flesh which smelled of ripe corn. How had she managed to get near them, to make them do all the things she claimed she had? Overcoming my shame, I stroked their black skin; the sun notwithstanding, it was as cool as water from a well.

At that moment, a bearded man with a crutch appeared at the car door with an old Turkish towel on his head for a turban, and a slipper in one hand. He was the school teacher. I had no business being there; no talking to pupils who had been punished! The *ulema*'s eyes were very nearly popping out of his head, dogs were barking, the shouting roused the whole neighbourhood. When he grabbed both children roughly by the arm and yanked them out of the car, I repressed an urge to break his crutch over his back, and drove home, feeling deeply uncomfortable.

LV

I HAD NO INTENTION of letting matters rest there. I had to be fully initiated, come what may.

At that point, I stooped very low; not being able, unaided, to find the royal road to orgiastic excess, I begged ... oh yes, I was not too ashamed to beg the favour of being made part of it. What possible reason could Clotilde have for refusing? These days women's lovers carry camaraderie to such extremes ... I wanted to be worthy of her wild ecstasies.

At this point, I have to declare one strange aspect of my behaviour which I have never been able to explain; until this day, it has always been absolutely incomprehensible to me. Clotilde didn't say no but returned a vague answer, dreamily, agreed, then put it off ... and went on covering her tracks.

So then, greatly daring, I offered her my services. As I went out late one day to catch the last collection, I'd spotted a couple of abandoned children sleeping head to tail on the steps of the post-office; could I get them to come with me?

I've already mentioned that our days and nights were two worlds which never coincided. It was out of the question for me to try any sort of casual approach by day, not even through oblique allusions, to a topic which occupied too many of my thoughts. So I waited for night and the hour when Clotilde was stalked by her demon, before I uncaged my plan, which I did in a voice roughened by unhealthy excitement.

"Bring those waifs here? Are you mad? What on earth would you do with them?"

"Well, first thing, I'd make them have a bath!"

"You have no feel for the sensual life," she said with a laugh, the laugh she always used now, it was like the *skreek* of a glazier's diamond on glass.

The thought that anyone could spice up moral degradation by adding physical depravity sent an icy shiver down my spine, but so far gone was I now that the thrill of excitement it gave me, plus all I was discovering that was new to my innocence, whipped me on until the blood flowed.

Corruption of appetite gained ground in me, slowly at times, at others moving like lightning, but always stealthily. When I became aware that I had crossed another line, it was already too late.

HECATE AND HER DOGS

In the end, I lost all sense of restraint. Proverbs 3 tells us: 'Give not thy strength unto women'. I had given mine. Infinitely vulnerable, I had been reduced to an apathetic, mindless, licentious jelly.

LVI

THERE COMES A MOMENT when events, arriving from various points of the compass, converge and block all exits; all you can do is stand back, mark time and await the verdict of destiny.

I had got up late and it was past noon when I reached the office. I was greeted with these words:

"The agent for Z's Bank was here and he wasn't best pleased. Said it was the third time he's put himself out, at your request, to speak to you about a business matter, and then he finds you're not in. He would like you to arrange a definite appointment for him, sir."

I did the rounds of the departments; the accounts clerk informed me there had been two large withdrawals of funds.

"What's in the mail?" I asked a Syrian I had taken on in a hurry to replace my right-hand man who had left following a rather disagreeable scene: he had asked for leave on the grounds that he was suffering from stress.

"Stress?" I'd snapped back testily. "There's not that much to do here and anyway I'm always around."

"Always?" he said sarcastically.

I'll admit that being worn out by sleepless nights, I was now coming less often to the bank: I only put in brief appearances. I thought this perfectly reasonable, given the fact that business was slack and local commerce sluggish.

"Last week, you weren't in at all," he had the impudence to add, "and your home number wasn't answering; it wasn't my fault if you couldn't be contacted. There was a blip on the New York market; I had to see to everything, take responsibility which was yours by rights ... I liquidated Monsieur Tartin. Too many long-term debts."

"You sold his shares in Antofagasta? But he was angling to be in the majority. Of all the tomfool ... "

"That does it, it's the last straw. Sir, I hereby withdraw my request for leave and have the honour to tender my resignation."

And so he left. To replace him, I'd come up with this Syrian.

"What's in the mail?"

"A letter from the Dutch Consul—an instruction to transfer the Dutch Consulate's account to the Bank of Balthazar Bendoub."

This was far more serious. Reasons can always be found to account for the calling in of monies—there had been quite a few instances of it in recent weeks—in a country like this where neither people nor capital hang around for ever. But the Dutch account was different.

I knew the Consul, name of Van den Plas; we used to go fishing together, especially at the beginning. I was pretty sure I'd find him on his sailing boat. I'd ask him to give me a lift back in his car and was confident I'd soon get the truth out of him.

Behind the wheel, the Dutchman, until then so affable, turned grim the moment I started asking questions; his nose asserted itself in the middle of his good-natured face, which made him look like the raven released from Noah's Ark. To avoid looking at me, he kept his eyes on the sand road off which the car might skid at any moment. His lower lip trembled slightly, as if he were about to speak, but he bit his tongue and said nothing.

"Surely," said I, "you haven't lost confidence in us? Our balance sheet is rock-solid, our positions copper-bottomed, our assets substantial … "

"I don't doubt it for a moment, but those strongboxes of yours, which use padlocks, must be a hundred years old. There are no vaults worthy of the name anywhere in town outside of Bendoub's Bank which has just imported an entire strong room from London: that's something which gives customers absolute security."

This reply, delivered with evident embarrassment, did not convince me. I felt pretty sure that if the Dutchman was taking his business elsewhere, it was to prevent the Consulate's financial affairs coming under scrutiny and even interference from the financial arm of the foreign country I represented.

Not for one moment did I suspect the truth.

LVII

You will find it hard to believe me when I add that, despite this warning shot across my bows, I made no changes in the way I lived my life. I continued to loiter in the most dubious places, practicing the lessons I had learnt from Clotilde, and showing not the slightest sign of originality in that outlandish field of endeavour. The long flights of steps, the covered walkways opening at intervals onto the sea-damp night, the deserted fishing boats, the alleys blue with moonlight, the steam baths, the Arab cafés, the scrap-metal market with its tacks and nails in heaps on planks of wood and petrol cans hammered flat into tin sheets, the patches of waste ground and the workshops where reed mats were woven and children crouched stitching espartograss artefacts with string—in all these places I became an all too common sight. Swirls of small girls artful as djinns, who were swatted away by pimps wielding pink Moroccan slippers, followed me around offering their services. I threw myself recklessly into the inescapable maelstrom of the passions with the same determination which others use to subdue them. I envied Clotilde, to whom wickedness came naturally, whereas I had to try so very hard to outdo her by committing acts of unbelievable folly.

LVIII

I HAD DEVISED an entire programme of misconduct for myself and followed it step by step. Throwing caution to the wind, I plunged into the quagmire, gleefully and up to my neck. I had eventually discovered exactly how to set about it, for I now had an eye for it, like an old fox. I was so bold, so callous, it scared me. Now I never missed my mark. I took no chances. I did not linger. I never stayed long at the scene of my actions but moved on elsewhere. In record time, I could select, entice, cajole my chosen game, lead them to slaughter, and then go looking for the next tasty morsel.

I began mixing with the cosmopolitan idle rich who crop up everywhere: splenetic titled Englishmen, Nordic mill-owners with morals as moveable as their yachts, grand Russian ladies whose religion was the only thing about them that was orthodox. Our centre of operations and supply base was the grand mansion of the correspondent of the largest American press agency (who would subsequently die by murder), a palace straight out of the *Arabian Nights*, paved with alabaster.

I was terrified of going there but could not stay away. I acquired a taste, which grew stronger by the day, for the anxiety which is a constant in a life of vice; certain of my more crapulous forays left me with my heart in my mouth and my stomach churning, like a man reading a crime serial in a newspaper. Terrorised by the thought of scandal, I savoured my angst—conscious displeasure, secret pleasure. The violence I did to my basically decent nature was almost certainly an inverted form of the self-denial so dear to Protestant hearts. "At last," I told myself, "fantasy has entered my life!"

But why linger over memories which come back to me now only because chance has redirected me to this place?

LXIX

CLOTILDE CONTINUED to elude me. Performing as actively as ever on the stage of her imagination by night, she continued to slip through my fingers by day. If I had her cornered by some line of questioning, she always contrived to find an escape route. I sensed that I was encircled by her cast of secondary characters and accomplices, but I still could not pin them down. They hid, they outran me and I lost the scent. If I chanced upon her surrounded by children, it seemed the most innocent thing in the world, whether she was switching on the radio for them, an almost unknown invention which filled them with wonder (they would crowd round and wait for "the music to swell up in the little house"), or taking them out on a picnic, slipping away in the crushing midday sun into the shade of a rock to roast lamb on a spit.

Was it a return to her childhood paradise, an attempt to resuscitate the past, or a need for a form of authority which could be placated by being allowed to control one small area of her life? Was she playing? If so, at what? At being a school teacher or Princess of Baghdad, the heroine of a novel or an ogress? Or was it simply that she had never grown up and merely occupied the body of an adult?

I was never invited to her dollies' tea parties. I felt I wasn't welcome, I dared not insist and actually took an odd sort of pleasure in being kept away; something within me secretly rejoiced at being held at arm's length.

I marvelled at her technique which was immensely more advanced than mine, and it was invisible, as with all great virtuosi. Clotilde's resolute, practical side never deserted her in even her wildest excesses. Her bold handling of risky ventures, the decisiveness she brought to her shameless desires, left me gasping. Whereas I, even at my most audacious, and despite all the progress I made, still clung to an evangelical, missionary streak in my character which was both tragic and farcical.

LX

THE HOUSE I RENTED was an old Arab palace, with cracked walls and a musty smell, dislocated paving stones and terraces buckled by upthrusting roots. A donkey turning in circles drew rust-coloured water from a well which was used to irrigate fields of arum lilies. Through the lattice windows, the sea, only a whit less blue than the tiles on the walls, cut a sharp line across the horizon at the point of infinity.

At night, I would climb up to one of my five terraces and gaze up at a sky sprinkled with stars. "What a contrast," I remarked to Clotilde, "between the workings of the universal mechanism and the mess made by men!"

"There speaks the Rousseau in you!"

A mess from which children are less absolved than we are, for they are closer to original sin. Having so much to do with them, I was now beginning to understand them. For the first time, I was seeing in their nakedness the young Arabs, Jews, and sometimes Europeans whom I brought home with me, and it was from them that I learnt about vice. They knew far more about it than I did. Whether beautiful or ill-favoured, they were versions of us, scaled down in physique but life-sized in passion, subtle, sensual savages, primitive monsters of hate and cunning, and infinitely superior to us in their experience of evil. They did not sink into it gradually, but embraced it with open arms. My philanthropic nature, my previous history would normally have inclined me to convert our encounters into an evening Sunday School. But if I ever proved remiss in my debauches, they soon called me to order. I was the innocent there. Their lubricity was immune from the guilt I felt so keenly, free of the pricks and qualms of my conscience. I hated myself for encouraging such guilty passions. Those children seized me by the coat tails and dragged me towards the brink.

Where was I heading? For a man to take such risks when he had no idea what he wanted verged on the ridiculous. Was it just me sinking into the quagmire or, sticking to my original plan, was I simply engaging in deviant behaviour so that I could rescue Clotilde from it? Was I spectator or player? The surgeon or the infected body?

LXI

A PATH DOWN THE CLIFF overlooking my house led to a cove which in summer attracted more people by night than by day. The townsfolk came there to bathe, set up fishing lines or just talk as they lay on the cool sand, waiting for the sunrise so that they could go home to bed. During the hottest times, there was a constant toing and froing of donkeys hauling seaweed, of fishermen carrying moray eels and skate, their bamboo poles slung across their shoulders.

That night, Clotilde was sleeping at my house, and from the terrace we could hear the denizens of the beach laughing, quarrelling, singing. Beneath this soundscape was the whisper of the advancing and retreating waves.

Clotilde was leaning over the salt-rusted iron balustrade, looking out over the sea. She had her back to me. Her hair, which she'd had cropped short on her neck in the new fashion, no longer hid her backbone with a skein of uncoiled silk. In the light cast by a lamp dimmed by a mantle of mayfly, I observed, without indulgence now, the nodules of her spine which protruded all the way from the nape of her neck to the small of her back.

If only the balustrade would give way ...

All the hate which collects in the lee of love was gratified by the thought; by ridding me of Clotilde would not her death cure me of the sickness I had caught from her?

"Don't lean over like that ... " I said, wishing that she would lean a great deal further.

The hotter our passions run, the less forgiving we become. This was my vengeance on her for being her passive slave, and I kept telling myself that it didn't mean a thing really. "I used to think she was beautiful in parts and ugly overall, but even confining myself to her parts, that knotted rope running down between those jutting shoulder-blades ... "

What was she thinking, with her chin resting on her folded arms? What did she know of the person I had turned into? I had kept everything hidden from her. Had she found me out? And, assuming that she knew all about my new experiments, which of the two Clotildes still took an interest in me, the day-She or the night-She? I was left totally helpless by this reversible creature.

Today, on the Rhine, there are still days and nights of carnival when the inhabitants of the straitest-laced towns are allowed staggering licence; when the body is disguised, the soul stripped bare emerges; respectable matrons under full sail navigate leaking sewers; and fat burghers take time off from a year of deep-dyed swindles by changing into werewolves. *Carni-val* means 'carnality prevails' …

In the same way did Clotilde bridge the gulf between hidden desire and the blatant, unapologetic act.

I had followed her down blind alleys where the senses were led astray by the wilful urgings of her head. On that evening, I again witnessed the slow awakening of her senses, but this time her excitement was not contagious. It enraged me to watch her pursuing her own pleasure.

I moved closer. She turned her head, held out her lips and between mine slid a flat, moist tongue, the tongue of a bitch.

I was at her mercy. A sudden eruption of anger and desire made me slip one arm around her neck … oh to put, in wrestling parlance, a headlock on her and throw her to the canvas!

I was astounded by the sudden depth of the hate I felt for her. Clotilde … I loathed the name which was so ill-suited to someone so clammy, so clinging, so cloudy.

Suddenly I grabbed her by the throat. How I would have loved to strangle her, rip the mask from her face!

I screamed:

"You are going to tell me where you take those children! Now!"

"Not on your life!"

She pushed my hands away, turned her head to one side with an irritated shrug, as though I were delaying the enjoyment of her pleasures.

I shook her roughly:

"I don't know if you do everything you talk about but I warn you, I'm a practical man. I don't go in for weird fantasising. I can afford fresh meat too. I'll go and get you some now!"

I straightened up, quickly threw on some clothes. Clotilde tried her very best to stop me, gently at first, and then with fury, grappling me with both hands and going for me with her nails. It was plain to see that she hated me too.

And I loathed her.

We were the two lips of the same wound.

"Not on your life!" I said, imitating her. "You like playing children's games? Then children's games are what you'll get!"

I rushed down the stairs several at a time, incandescent with a rage to which action gave wings. My car stood waiting for me. My headlamps suddenly lit up the white walls of the street which had no windows only recesses for doors studded with bronze nails.

I did not take long to gather in my harvest. A quarter-of-an-hour later, I was back on the terrace, followed by the patter of small, bare feet.

Clotilde was not there.

LXII

On my desk, a letter which, in all the excitement, had escaped my attention—the judge who sat in the commercial court wanted me to go to see him.

The judge, a Scot named Kirkpatrick, had always shown me nothing but kindness. He was a likeable man, but I thought him ambiguous and overly fond of euphemisms. Basically, having neither range nor depth, he was a kind of mathematical point in the landscape and, as such, a person of some importance.

He greeted me pleasantly, sat me down in his big, scarlet morocco armchair and gave me whisky from Gibraltar. He began by discussing his health then, having drunk to mine, he told me he thought I was looking under the weather.

"You've been out here two years, my dear Spitzgartner. Two years without going back can be devilishly debilitating. I can't help thinking that it's high time you breathed the air of your native heath."

There was in fact a time when I had fully intended to ask for leave, but for months now I had given up thinking about it.

"I'll give it some thought," I said, "in the autumn … "

The judge refilled my glass with another, threatening whisky.

"If I were you, I wouldn't wait," he said (his circumspection was now braced with a dash of firmness). "Far better to move on before the bad weather sets in. That way, you avoid all sorts of aggravation … "

"Move on?" I said, taken aback.

He cut me short:

"We'll be sorry to lose you," he went on, switching from familiarity to high formality. "Many businesses, including some British, might suffer as a result but, from your point of view, I'm afraid it might well be a good idea if you started looking for another posting. It would be most advisable, yes, highly advisable."

"I don't see anything that might make me want … "

"You don't see it? That's a pity. The rumours circulating just now are the reason for the advice I've just given you … as a friend. You must believe me when I say that the European colony, and myself first and foremost, would have much preferred to keep one of its most brilliant members here. It's true, is it not, that you are consulted by a good many people in town?"

I pretended I didn't understand.

"There is nothing to these rumours. My bank has no grounds for complaint."

"Let's leave your bank out of it."

"Sir, you are picking a quarrel with the wrong man. Have I broken any of your rules? After all, this isn't Europe!"

Knowing that Muslim law does not recognise minors, I thought I was on safe ground. No one was going to haul me up before the Cadi.

The judge's features froze with the effort he was obliged to make to set generalities aside and enter that forbidden zone so loathed by Anglo-Saxons, the rubric headed: 'Personal Remarks'. He nevertheless decided to tackle matters head on. An Italian woman, a student … The Evangelical Mission wished to lodge a formal complaint. Had I forgotten that certain native families came under the protection of various consulates? The patrons of the Brasserie, headquarters of the Socialist Party, would not pass up a chance of bagging a banker.

"I am responsible for upholding moral standards in this place … " the judge said in conclusion. "There's far too much living cheek by jowl here."

To these last words, I responded with a smile, but I went home feeling that the wind had been taken out of my sails. I had always been a credit to my family and my education, that went without saying, in the way a man always honours a draft drawn on his bank. But today I had been declared bankrupt. Having so many times felt foolishly and falsely ashamed of myself, I had now come face to face with the real thing.

Throughout the entire conversation, Clotilde's name had not come up once. No one even suspected her.

LXIII

A FEW DAYS LATER, I got a letter from Paris. Head Office advised me most opportunely of a post as receiver which had been created in the Commercial Bank of China. I was urged to move to Peking.

I hated the idea of leaving Africa, but staying was out of the question—it would have meant moral and material ruin. So I accepted, body racked but heart comforted by the thought that Clotilde would soon follow me.

I rushed round and put it to her. A month would be long enough to close up her house. No one would be surprised that she was going to China. Saying she was going away to be near her husband would be the perfect excuse. She agreed.

I left.

She never came.

LXIV

I took an inordinate time to mend. I had been badly bruised by the recoil of the shot that had struck me, devastated by a love which gave no second chances, nor could it, for love now had no object. The conscious mind may forget, but the unconscious never forgets, is proof against all diversions. Each night I returned to the scene of my vilest deeds where, among the spirits from the deep, Clotilde rose up in my dreams. For a long time, I would wake with a start, filled with foreboding and simultaneously with desire, a desire to see Hecate spit out her dogs the way wicked witches spit out serpents, through the mouth. Love grows too close to the dung-heap not to carry a whiff of it on its breath.

The first year of my time in China was purgatory. It was as if I were being crushed under the weight of the heaviest things in the world—waiting and shame. I was not in control of my nerves, they were in charge of me, I felt as though my arms and legs were about to jump out of their sockets; twenty years on and I still have facial twitches which date from that time. A ruin among the ruins of a ruinous continent, I saw my own reflection in all the shattered bridges, burst dykes, wrecked railway tracks, and immobilised locomotives.

I was saved by my decline into mindlessness, my sensibilities entered full hibernation mode. I took on the most thankless tasks, checking accounts, writing up the minutes of committee meetings which the requirement to recast them into Chinese made even more tedious.

I did not ask for leave, I carried out the dreariest duties, I came up with no intelligent initiatives, all of which earned me the good opinion of the Bank's higher echelons. Having fully expected to discover all backs turned against me, I was amazed to find every hand extended. My horizons widened. I was entrusted with looking into town-based deficits and then province-wide embezzlement; until the day when, back for good in the land of the living, I could show what I was really made of and again become a first-rate professional. I swapped the Chinese abacus for an American calculating machine. Various states consulted me and asked for my advice.

These financial therapies, in which I specialised, speeded up my moral rebirth. I applied hot poultices to all wounds, including my own. I had obeyed a Chinese injunction dating from the time of the great plagues: "Go away quickly; flee far; come back slowly".

LXV

I stopped hurting; I stopped waiting. The Mediterranean salmagundi which had almost done for me receded into the past. I became acclimatised to Asia where the Great War stubbornly refused to end: Reds went on shooting Whites, communist commissars tortured lamas, Czechs rode roughshod over the entrails of Ostiaks and Samoyeds in their efforts to carve a route to the Pacific. The group, of which I was now a manager, steered a careful course between these hazards; it subsidised serfs who were tyrants or gave financial backing to overlords who were slaves.

So it came as no surprise to me when I was sent north, as part of a joint mission to negotiate a loan which had been requested by some Russian cut-throat or other.

LXVI

THE EVENING OF MY ARRIVAL, I got my interview with Admiral Krubin in the railway saloon car he used as his base. Among his staff, among the Officer-instructors and accredited air pilots in his entourage, I noticed a French lieutenant colonel heavily decorated with palm-leaves and medals.

Once the business of the loan was out of the way (all the Admiral had to offer by way of security was thousands of acres of despair and peat-bog), the French Colonel was delegated to look after me. I was given his name—he was Clotilde's husband.

He had appeared at his appointed hour, boots smoking, through the steam of tea-cups, like a general out of Chinese folklore stalking the traveller who has wandered onto some battlefield dating from the Han dynasty. My past assumed human shape and rose to meet me.

We stayed behind by ourselves in the railway carriage. All around us, the wind swept the vast Asiatic desert which lay at the junction of the roads to Turkestan and Mongolia. The dust got the better of the double windows, settled on the plates, clouded the wine glasses and hung a red halo over my spectacles—through it I could barely make out Clotilde's husband.

Did he know? Did he feel as intensely about me as I did about him? Perhaps my name rang no bells? Men often approach the same woman by digging adjoining, parallel tunnels of which only the woman in question has the plan—provided, that is, she does forget or lose it.

How on earth had I imagined that this Officer-instructor could possibly have initiated Clotilde into the science of love? He wasn't even capable of briefing me on the region's coal-fields … His lack of curiosity was comprehensive. He didn't ask me about Europe, or Versailles, or Clemenceau. In his company, as the evening wore on, I began to lose all sense of time and place.

The man before me bore no resemblance to the photograph I had found, all that time ago, in Africa, in the pocket of his jacket. He was one of those doughty misfits, gaunt of face, who are thrown up by wars and, when the show's over, have no idea where to go.

We went outside. Above the rainless hurricane stars were shining and the wind, summoned to a Devils' wassail, seemed to be blowing down a human thigh-bone.

The Colonel led the way carrying my case in one hand and, with exquisite courtesy, lit my steps with the other in which he held an electric torch.

"You'll have to excuse the quarters."

A bunk had been made up for me opposite his in the Trans-Siberian sleeper. The billet of this ascetic man was full of storage batteries, binoculars, guns, bottles, Tibetan manuscripts. Above the bed, in a soap-box converted into shelves, was a row of books: *Louis Lambert*, *La Vie de Rancé*, *The Mechanism of Sexual Deviation*.

I bagged one bunk, he lay down on the other. He did not fall asleep any more than I did. He never took his eyes off me. Was he beginning to sense the presence of Clotilde, there, between us?

The need to make him talk consumed me:

"Aren't you thinking of going back to Europe?"

"No. Why?"

"To see ... your family?"

He didn't answer.

"Life's starting up again in Europe," I said. "And you're here, twiddling your thumbs."

He gave a sniggering sort of laugh:

"I'm paying my debts."

"Gambling debts?"

"Debts from the Big Game."

"What do you mean?"

"Wicked deeds ... stains on body and soul."

"That goes for all of us."

He turned a look on me which stopped me in my tracks.

"Not you. You've been delivered from all that. I'm still waiting …" (He began to laugh.) "I mean I'm waiting to be demobilised. When I am, if ever I am, and the world does not follow Russia's example and stay on a footing of permanent mobilisation … "

He stopped.

"When you're demobbed," I persisted, "what course do you intend to follow?"

He sat up on his pillow.

"The only course open to me, the path to Knowing," he replied curtly.

The night wore on. The French officer became unreal; a brief-candled projection by a shaman who objectifies the pictures in his head …

It was an effort to speak:

"So you're not intending to travel?"

"The only kind of travelling left to a man who has left illusion behind him, is done in trances."

And he turned his face to the wall and turned off the light.

LXVII

I DID NOT SEE CLOTILDE AGAIN until 1942, in New York. It was at an official dinner and I had been placed next to her.

Outwardly, she hadn't changed much. She carried her fifty years like one of those ever-young ageing American women. The effect of the years had merely been to fix her once fluid features and leave internal wrinkles which no amount of massage can smooth; her light voice had dropped a full register, had become characterless; she spoke French with an English accent and English with a French accent, and both to stunning perfection; her persona, so relaxed and composed even down to the way she held her profile, no longer trailed wisps of sultriness. Observing her elegant, condescending manners, you knew she had acquired social rank. She was in charge of some sort of war work. There seemed nothing left, beneath that hard, glossy shell, of the secret part of her which had wrecked my life. She was like the diamonds which, having no memory of the millions of centuries they spent buried in the earth, of the intestines of the Negro in which they were hidden, the sticky fingers of the usurer, the robberies, the murders, the spoliations of which they had been the cause, finally sit in triumph on the brow of the victor, with sparkling disdain.

I thought that no reference would be made to the past; a table of fifty guests is hardly the venue for settling old scores. But Clotilde plunged in, head first, maybe because she found an hour's silence too much to bear, or else simply because there was somewhere deep in her worldly soul a magnificent capacity for amnesia and new starts.

She spoke at length of her social activities, the praise showered on her for it, and then turning graciously to me:

"I gather that you too have become a person of importance," she began. "I have such good memories of you."

"I don't of you, Clotilde. Perhaps I loved you too much … It took me fifteen years to get over it. And even now there are times when I turn into a haunted house which generates its own ghosts."

I spoke without giving our fellow guests a second thought, without wondering if they understood French. It took a great deal of effort to look her straight in the eye.

She held my look; with a hand ungloved to the wrist she pushed her glass away:

"It must be said, my dear, that you were exceedingly depraved … " she said calmly.

No sooner had Clotilde delivered herself of this appalling rejoinder than everyone rose from table. She took one step forward. I seized her arm and gripped it roughly; it was time at last that I got my answer.

"Clotilde, wait … I have one other thing to say to you. You're not going to get away from me again."

She halted, surprised, offended.

"In China, I met someone … "

I was as cold-blooded as the executioner who stands with axe aloft.

"That's right, in China, I met a man, and you know who."

She shied away and began to tremble. Then her face creased into a scowl, her eyes turned green and I beheld Hecate.

Vevey 1953

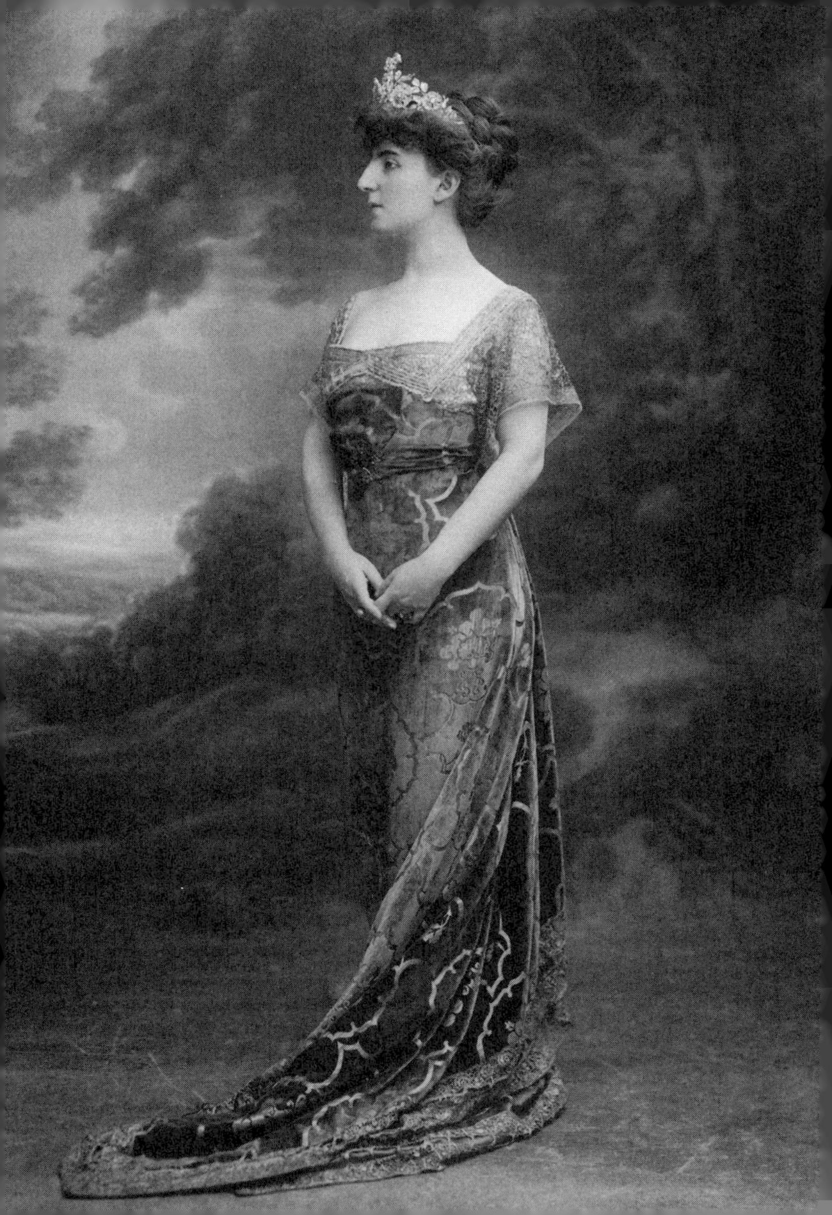

A TANGIER AFTERWORD

A strait-laced Calvinist who, in a city of vice, meets a real harlot, and with her his ruin; the charm of this dreadful 1920s woman and her pronounced penchant for dark little rascals, for the black boys who 'melt in the mouth' like milk chocolate; the love story between the two, or rather the classic descent into the hell of sexual desire; a most traditional exotic setting—the pinnacle of late nineteenth-century orientalist knick-knacks—this is why *Hécate et ses chiens* could be thought as a *roman de gare* for prurient chamber-maids and horny lieutenants. And yet it isn't. This short book, which one could read in twenty-five minutes, is a masterpiece of camp. The dissembling tone of the protagonist and first-person narrator, the progressive revelation, with masterful strokes by the author, of the lady's secret habits (*Hecate and her Puppies* might have been a more appropriate title) makes it so. It is a masterpiece because of the way the language—a polished, naive and neoclassical language, almost dusty with chalk—adapts to some of the most disturbing descriptions of sex in the history of literature, making the author's coevals and fellow-nationals Genet, Jouhandau, Cocteau and Gide look like writers for school girls. It is a masterpiece because of the constant omissions, the candid and malicious admissions, the silences—Tangier, for example, the city where the story is played out (and the only one where it could have been played out), is never named.

Nothing could be more mistaken than to seek in a novel links with its author's life (unless it is Proust's biographer George Painter who is doing so). But the reference to Helen from Goethe's *Faust* in the epigraph at the beginning of the novel is too tempting! After a 'bad war' the Morands found themselves exiled in Tangier—like so many others. We think of the second '*belle Hélène*' (the first being Helen of Troy and the third, obviously, the incomparable Madame Rochas), Hélène Soutzo, Madame Morand herself, a bit of a Brancovan-Bibesco, a friend of Proust, getting bored on her own with her husband in a provincial city. Without the Ritz and without Dior, without gossip and without people to see (apart from the occasional fervent collaborationist like Marga d'Andurain, borrowed from the pages of the wonderful early novels of Modiano: will the Morands have socialised with her? Known her? Met her?), abandoned in a sleepy little town that still echoed with the riding crops of Caid McLean and the groans of Walter Harris at the hands of the bandit Raisuni and his brutal Djebala henchmen, a dirty Arab city, pre-Paul Bowles-Barbara Hutton-David Herbert (not by chance does Morand set his novel about his stay in the city with his wife a good twenty years before), an anteroom-city in which a dropsical, half-dotty Sultan kept the foreigners waiting before receiving them in Fez, at a court 'dressed up' like a funfair imagined by Diane Arbus—a city in which it was also almost always too hot to wear sable and panther and astrakhan toques. *La belle Hélène* Soutzo must have been in a terrible mood in that little house by the sea, now demolished, at the foot of a fashionable orphanage and the former Scott house (now the residence of the King of Qatar). Just imagine, Hélène Soutzo aglitter in Schiaparelli and Vionnet and early Fulco di Verdura, having dinner with the absent-minded Lady Scott (recently arrived from India, perhaps in flat sandals)? Or Hélène at tea with Marthe de Chambrun Ruspoli (she too suspected of collaboration, as well as of archaeological *sorcellerie*)—the unmissable meeting between the two, with Ruspoli blathering about the survival of cults of Isis among the Berber population, and Soutzo—like São Schlumberger at a dinner in Tangier forty years later, speaking of the pretentious Italian woman who asked her in order to break the ice: "Do you prefer the sculptures of Northern or Southern India?"—São raising her eyes to the sky with a great flash of emerald drop earrings that had once belonged to the Maharani of Baroda: '*Mais qu'est-ce qu'elle raconte?*' Is it possible to imagine Hélène in the souk? *La belle Hélène* at Spartel? At the Caves of Hercules? In Manolo's lair, peering out from behind a mirror, as *chez* Jupien? Hélène, the epitome of Parisian chic, playing canasta with some little *collabo* madam in a pine-marten stole?

Sour and furious, Hélène turns her consort's life into a kind of hell; she complains constantly, won't go out, can't go on, yells, bangs her head against the wall; hates the sea and the palms and the Arabs and the *bronzage* and the East wind and all those fags … *Monsieur*, ex-Ambassador of Pétain first in Romania (where she had at least some family) then in Berne (a stone's throw from everywhere), *monsieur*, in the doghouse, suffers and nurses his revenge. It amuses me to think that there is a lot of *la belle Hélène* in our Clotilde/Hécate—her chic, the snake of vertebrae down her spine, her haughty manners, her occasional Slavic harshness, her big feet. Perhaps not the little boys: but who knows, such was the boredom …

This little page, of course, is merely a Tangerine joke.

UMBERTO PASTI
Tangier 2009